STEPS TO REA

Dear Parent:

Congratulations! Your child is taking the first steps on an exciting journey. **The destination? Independent reading!**

STEPS TO READING will help your child get there. The programme offers three steps to reading success. Each step includes fun stories and colourful art, and the result is a complete literacy programme with something for every child.

Learning to Read, Step by Step!

1 **Start to Read   Nursery – Preschool**
• **big type and easy words** • **rhyme and rhythm** • **picture clues**
For children who know the alphabet and are eager to begin reading.

2 **Let's read together   Preschool – Year 1**
• **basic vocabulary** • **short sentences** • **simple stories**
For children who recognise familiar words and sound out new words with help.

3 **I can read by myself   Years 1-3**
• **engaging characters** • **easy-to-follow plots** • **popular topics**
For children who are ready to read on their own.

STEPS TO READING is designed to give every child a successful reading experience. The year levels are only guides. Children can progress through the steps at their own speed, developing confidence in their reading, no matter what their year.

Remember, a lifetime love of reading starts with a single step!

By John Winskill
Illustrated by the Disney Global Artists

This edition published by Parragon in 2011

Parragon
Queen Street House
4 Queen Street
Bath BA1 1HE, UK

Based on the Mowgli stories in *The Jungle Book* and *The Second Jungle Book* by
Rudyard Kipling.

ISBN 978-1-4454-2107-0

Printed in Malaysia

Jungle Friends

Bath · New York · Singapore · Hong Kong · Cologne · Delhi
Melbourne · Amsterdam · Johannesburg · Auckland · Shenzhen

Mowgli lives in
the jungle.
He has lots of friends.

Furry friends.

Scaly friends.

Feathered friends.

Giant friends.

Mowgli has fun with
his jungle friends.

Every day they
march and play.

They run.

They swing.

They eat.

They dance.

But of all his
jungle friends . . .

Big Baloo is his favourite.

Baloo loves his
"Little Buddy."

And Mowgli loves Baloo.

Now turn
over for the
next story...

By Apple Jordan
Illustrated by Robbin Cuddy

Ðisney

T H E
LION KING
Bug Stew

PaRRagon

Bath • New York • Singapore • Hong Kong • Cologne • Delhi
Melbourne • Amsterdam • Johannesburg • Auckland • Shenzhen

Timon and Pumbaa
love bugs.
Yum!

Simba learns to
like them, too.

Time to hunt
for more bugs!

The friends go and
find a few.

They look under rocks.

They look up in trees.

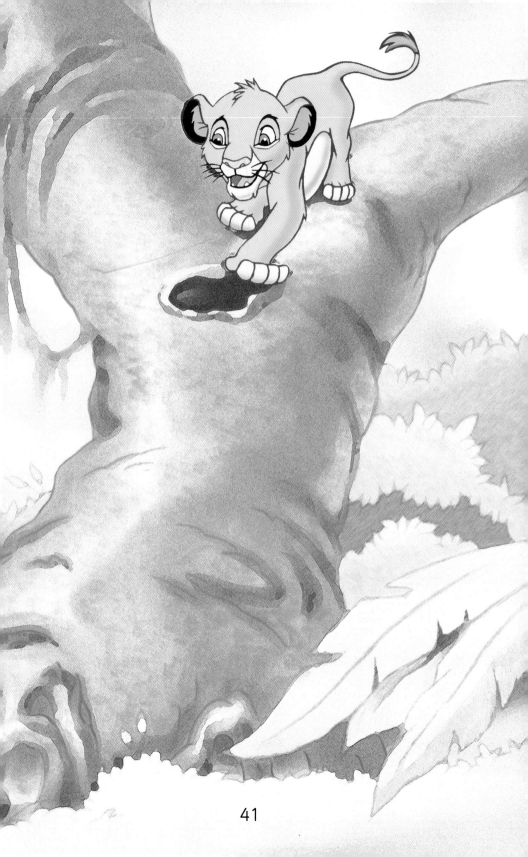

They find fat flies.

They find bumblebees.

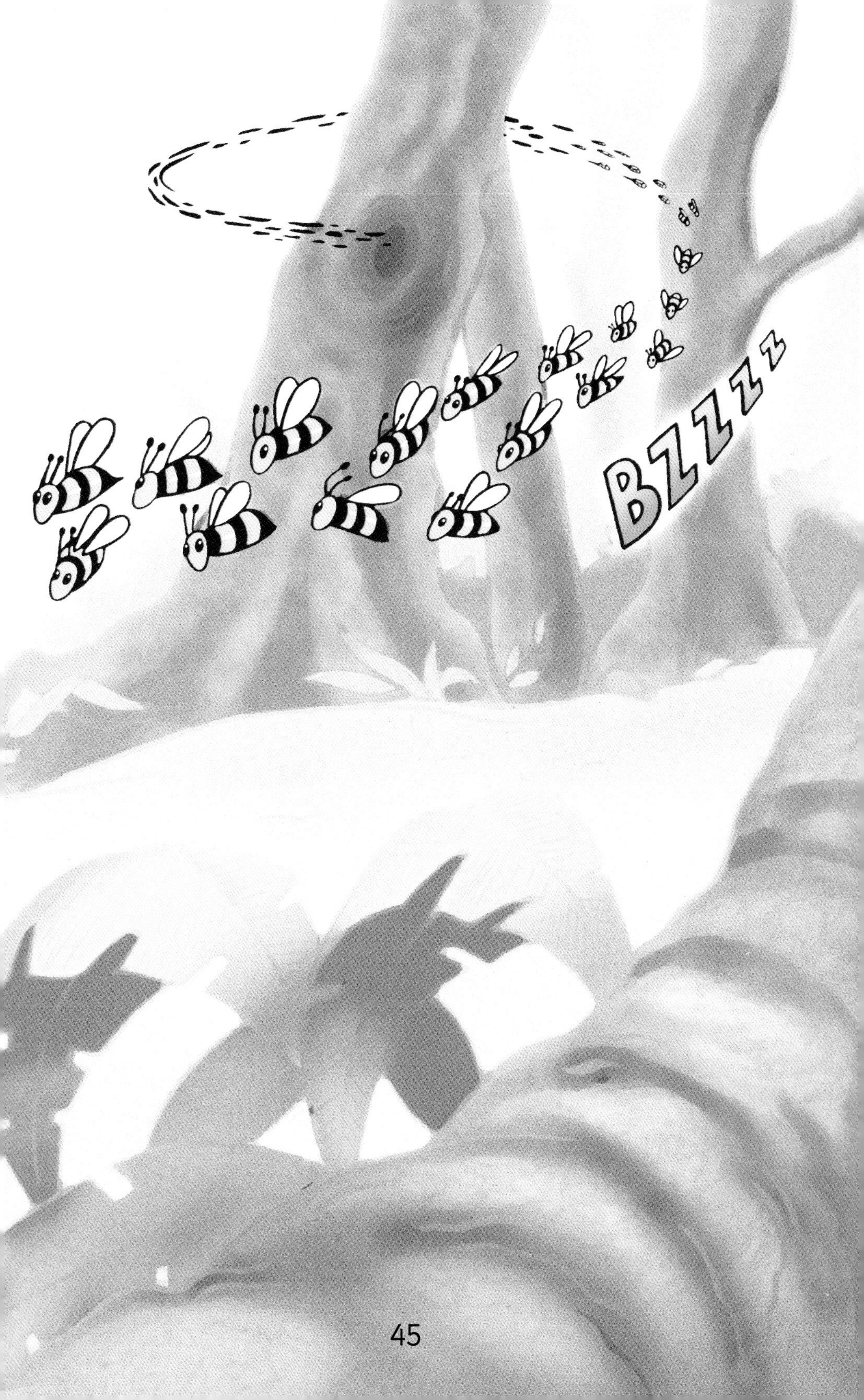
BZZZZZ

They look inside logs
for slimy slugs.

They look and they look
for all types of bugs.

Big bugs
and little bugs.

Fuzzy, furry,
wiggly bugs.

Crunchy bugs,
sticky bugs.
Chewy, gooey,
icky bugs.

CRUNCH

51

Bugs that can sting.

Bugs that hop high.

Bugs with big wings.

Bugs that can fly.

Bugs that run fast.

Bugs that crawl slow.

Bugs that can swim.

Bugs that can glow.

They have
buckets of bugs.
Now what will they do?

Mix them all up

and make a bug stew!